Lissy's Friends

Grace Lin

Viking

To my friends the blue rose girls.

—G.L.

Lissy was the new girl at school.

Nobody talked to her.

Nobody smiled at her.

At the playground, Lissy stood on the merry-go-round by herself.

Because Lissy ate lunch alone, she was finished before lunchtime was over. Since she didn't have anything else to do, Lissy took the lunch menu in front of her and began to fold it. Soon, she had made a little paper crane.

"Hello," Lissy said to the paper crane. "I will call you Menu, and you will be my friend."

And to her surprise, Menu opened its eyes and blinked at her. Menu looked to the right, then to the left, and fluttered up with its paper wings.

The rest of the day, Lissy smiled a secret smile.

"Did you make any friends in school today?" Mommy asked when Lissy came home.

"Well," Lissy said, patting Menu in her pocket, "I did make one friend."

"Good," Mommy said. "I'm sure you'll make more tomorrow."

And she did. The next day, Lissy made lots of friends.

Her friends went with her . . .

everywhere.

And Lissy was never alone.

One day, Lissy heard a group of kids laughing as they went down the street. They stopped at one house and then another, but they didn't stop at Lissy's.

"Lissy," Mommy called from downstairs, "why don't you go with your friends to the playground? I think they are all headed that way."

Lissy looked at her paper friends.

"Yes," she said. "Let's go to the playground."

Lissy led her friends down the street and to the playground.

"We'll ride the merry-go-round first," she told them. "Then we can all ride together."

So all the paper animals crowded onto the merry-go-round, and Lissy began to push it. Round and round Lissy pushed. She ran so hard she didn't see that her friends were having a difficult time staying on . . .

SWOOSH! The paper giraffe flew! Then the paper elephant and the rabbit!

A strong wind caught
them and carried them up
into the sky.

When Lissy jumped on, the merry-go-round was empty! She looked up and saw her paper friends flying away.

"No! Come back!" Lissy cried.

But they couldn't.

"No more friends," Lissy said, and she sat down on the merry-go-round and covered her face with her hands.

"Hey, is this yours?" a voice said.

Lissy looked up. There was a girl holding a paper crane. Menu!

"It's neat," the girl said. "Did you make it?"

Lissy looked at the girl. She was smiling at her. Lissy nodded.

"Can you show me how?" the girl asked. "I'm Paige."

Paige came over to Lissy's house, and Lissy showed her how to make a paper crane. Then they made a paper fox and dragonfly. They talked and laughed.

And the next day, Paige pushed Lissy on the merry-go-round with lots and lots of friends.

Dear Lissy,

We hope you are doing
well. We are having fun
traveling the world. We
miss you!

♡ your friends

P.s. Tell Menu Hello!

Lissy Lin
58 Paper Place
Valley Fold, MA
10000

Viking

Published by Penguin Group

Penguin Young Readers Group, 345 Hudson Street, New York, New York 10014, U.S.A.

Penguin Group (Canada), 90 Eglinton Avenue East, Suite 700, Toronto, Ontario, Canada M4P 2Y3 (a division of Pearson Penguin Canada Inc.)

Penguin Books Ltd, 80 Strand, London WC2R 0RL, England

Penguin Ireland, 25 St Stephen's Green, Dublin 2, Ireland (a division of Penguin Books Ltd)

Penguin Group (Australia), 250 Camberwell Road, Camberwell, Victoria 3124, Australia (a division of Pearson Australia Group Pty Ltd)

Penguin Books India Pvt Ltd, 11 Community Centre, Panchsheel Park, New Delhi – 110 017, India

Penguin Group (NZ), 67 Apollo Drive, Mairangi Bay, Auckland 1310, New Zealand (a division of Pearson New Zealand Ltd.)

Penguin Books (South Africa) (Pty) Ltd, 24 Sturdee Avenue, Rosebank, Johannesburg 2196, South Africa

Penguin Books Ltd, Registered Offices: 80 Strand, London WC2R 0RL, England

First published in 2007 by Viking, a division of Penguin Young Readers Group

1 3 5 7 9 10 8 6 4 2

LIBRARY OF CONGRESS CATALOGING-IN-PUBLICATION DATA

Lin, Grace.

Lissy's friends / by Grace Lin.

p. cm.

Summary: Lissy is the new girl at school and very shy, so she makes origami friends to keep her company.

ISBN 978-0-670-06072-6 (hardcover)

[1. Origami—Fiction. 2. Bashfulness—Fiction. 3. Friendship—Fiction. 4. Schools—Fiction.] I. Title.

PZ7.L644Lis 2007   [E]—dc22   2006031029

Manufactured in China

Set in Century Expanded

Book design by Nancy Brennan

How to fold a paper crane

1
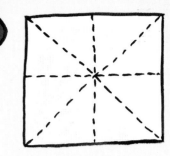
fold and unfold along lines shown

5

6
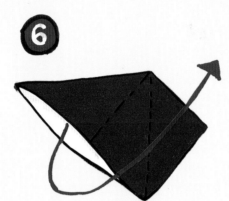

7

11
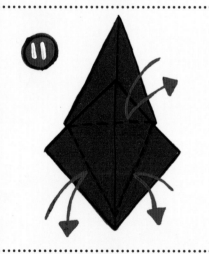

12
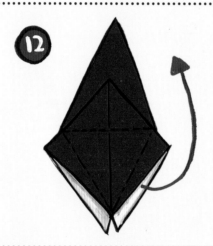

13

fold top layer only

17

fold up and inside to make tail

18

fold down and inside to make head

19

pull wings outward